The Case of the
Sabotaged School Play

Another Sam and Dave Mystery Story

Leroy Is Missing

The Case of the

Sabotaged
School Play

—◆—

Marilyn Singer

ILLUSTRATED BY

JUDY GLASSER

Harper & Row, Publishers

New York

Thanks to Joe Morton and Jim Perpich
for technical assistance

The Case of the Sabotaged School Play
Text copyright © 1984 by Marilyn Singer
Illustrations copyright © 1984 by Judy Glasser
For information address
Harper & Row, Publishers, Inc., 10 East 53rd Street,
New York, N.Y. 10022. Published simultaneously in
Canada by Fitzhenry & Whiteside Limited, Toronto.

Library of Congress Cataloging in Publication Data
Singer, Marilyn.
    The case of the sabotaged school play.

    Summary: A boring school play becomes big news when
sabotage is suspected.
    [1. Mystery and detective stories   2. Plays—Fiction]
I. Glasser, Judy, ill.   II. Title.
PZ7.S6172Cas 1984   [Fic]   83-48437
ISBN 0-06-025794-6
ISBN 0-06-025795-4 (lib. bdg.)

Designed by Constance Fogler
1 2 3 4 5 6 7 8 9 10
First Edition

The Case of the

Sabotaged School Play

1

"'Sink me, if it's not Jean La Fleet, the pirate king,'" Mary Ellen Moseby read in a bad British accent.

Dave Bean stifled a yawn. Mary Ellen's plays always put him to sleep. He wouldn't be in them— or the Drama Club for that matter—if he didn't like to act so much. Acting was great. Putting on a false nose, a wig, a tunic, a sword. Standing on stage in front of an audience. Dave loved it. He even thought he might become an actor when he grew up. That is, if he didn't become a private eye.

Mary Ellen switched to an equally awful French accent. "'The same. And your weesh, Sir Hugo, is my command. Gentlemen, sink zis sheep.'"

Joel Mazzara, president of the Drama Club, turned to Dave and whispered, not very quietly, "*Baaaa.*"

Mary Ellen's already pink skin turned pinker. Her upturned nose pointed to the ceiling as she said, in a snooty voice, "The trouble with you, Joel Mazzara, is that you have no taste."

Joel stood up, hands on his hips. "Well, then, there must be a lot of other people who don't either, because nobody ever comes to see your plays except the parents of the kids who are in them." He sighed and changed his tone. "Look, Mary Ellen, you can write all right, but people don't want to see stuff like this. It's corny." He turned to the rest of the club. "What I think we should do is tell Ms. Kirby we want to put on a famous musical. Something that everyone will like. Something like *Grease*."

Grease! The kids in the club began to murmur excitedly. "I wanna be Danny." "You'd be great as Sandy." "How about Donna as Rizzo?" "My brother has this T-shirt I could wear."

Dave was excited too. "I could slick my hair back and wear a leather jacket and Mom couldn't even complain," he said to Sam.

Sam grinned and nodded. He was shyer than Dave and went in more for sports than acting. But he was thinking that if they put on *Grease* even he might ask Ms. Kirby, the director, if he could be in it, instead of working the lights as usual. It would be fun to jump around on a hot rod and act tough.

Then, a thin blond girl named Ginger Janowitz piped up, "Ms. Kirby won't let us put on *Grease*. You all know she thinks we should perform plays that students have written instead. Besides, I like Mary Ellen's play. I think it's...original."

"Well, I don't," Donna Jordan put in. "I think Joel's right. *The Merry Pirates* is—"

"A very fine play," a grown-up voice said.

All heads turned to the doorway. Standing there

4

was Ms. Kirby, the drama teacher and director of the play. "Now, I know some of you have been disappointed about the size of the audiences for our last productions, but I'm sure with a little more publicity, we'll get a full—well, a fuller—house this time. Mary Ellen's put a lot of work into this play and we are going to put it on."

"Not if I can help it," Dave heard Joel mutter.

Other people sighed and shifted uncomfortably in their seats.

"I've chosen the cast," Ms. Kirby went on. "Joel, you will play Jean La Fleet. Dave, you'll be Sir Hugo. Donna will play Brigitte De Tour and Mary Ellen will be Brigitte's maid, Fifi. Jim, Sharon, Andy, Steve, Ron, Mike and Lois will be the pirates and Sir Hugo's crew."

"But Ms. Kirby, you didn't mention me," Ginger Janowitz called out.

"I'm sorry, Ginger. There aren't any other roles. But you—and everyone else who didn't get a part— can work on sets, costumes or the props. We all have to pitch in to make this the best production we've ever had. Here are your scripts. See you tomorrow for the first rehearsal."

Ginger got up to leave, and as she passed Donna, she gave her a nasty look. Joel did the same to Mary Ellen, who had stopped smiling and appeared lost in thought.

Dave turned to Sam. "Whew, I have a feeling this play isn't going to go so smoothly." Sam nodded.

But neither one of them knew just how much trouble there was going to be.

2

Dave was the first one to arrive for the rehearsal. A tall, red-faced man was waiting outside the door, which opened to reveal Ginger Janowitz. She jumped when she saw Dave.

"Oh, hi," she said. Then she turned to the red-faced man. "Ms. Kirby's not here, Dad."

Ginger's father turned to Dave. "Young man, have you seen Ms. Kirby?" he asked.

"She might be in the faculty room," answered Dave.

Mr. Janowitz said to his daughter, "Come on, Ginger. Let's look there. Now, don't worry. Be polite and persistent. And if that fails, remember, I'm on the school board and I'll tell her where to get off if she won't give you a part in this play."

They left. Dave shook his head. Mary Ellen was next to show up. "Did you read your script last night, Dave?" she asked.

"I...uh...looked through it," Dave said. "It was...interesting."

"Interesting. People say that when they don't like something."

For once, Dave was at a loss for words. Donna Jordan came sauntering into the room, with Joel Mazzara right behind her, as he usually was. The tiny beaded braids covering Donna's head bounced as she walked. Joel tugged one. "Oh, Brigitte, you look ravishing," Joel said.

Donna gave him a funny look. "Huh?"

"That's what my father always says to my mother."

"And I thought *my* parents were strange," Donna said. She looked around. "Where's Ms. Kirby? If we're really gonna put on this mess, we might as well get start.... Oh, 'scuse me, Mary Ellen, I didn't know you were here."

Clutching the big shoulder bag she always carried, Mary Ellen frowned. The rest of the cast began to wander in. Dave glanced out the window. The baseball team was practicing and Sam was up at bat. He turned his head, saw Dave and waved. Dave waved back. He watched as Sam swung and connected with the ball. A triple. Dave applauded his brother.

"At least there aren't any snakes in this play," Dave heard Joel say. He turned to look at him. "I can think of a few people who don't care much for snakes," Joel continued.

"Oh, shut up," said Donna.

Some of the other kids laughed. Dave smiled.

"There should be a parrot though," said a boy named Andy. "Pirates have parrots."

"That's a stereotype," Mary Ellen said.

Donna rolled her eyes.

Finally Ms. Kirby arrived. "Sorry I'm late. Something came up."

Some*one*, Dave said to himself, thinking of Ginger and her father.

"Mary Ellen, tell us a little about why you wrote this play and how you envision it performed," said Ms. Kirby.

Mary Ellen went to the front of the room and explained how she'd always loved pirate movies and how she'd decided to write a pirate play full of action and romance. "I think it should be performed seriously—not like it's silly," she said. "And we should have a real-looking set and use lots of special effects—strobe lighting, cannon sounds..."

"We're getting a little ahead of ourselves, Mary Ellen," interrupted Ms. Kirby. "But since you know so much about stage design, lighting and sound, Mr. Matthius, who'll be the art director, and I will be sure to consult with you when the time comes."

Donna let out a big sigh. "Can we start reading this aloud now?"

"All right," said Ms. Kirby.

Knapsacks, handbags, briefcases rustled as the actors pulled out their scripts. "I left mine in my desk last night," Donna said.

"You should have brought it home to read," said Ms. Kirby.

Donna went over to her desk and stuck her hand inside. She pulled out the script. With it came something long, skinny and scaly. Donna screamed at the top of her lungs and dropped the script and the scaly thing on the ground. It was a snake. Donna tried to run out of the room, but Ms. Kirby grabbed her. Dave was up in a bound. Joel doubled up laughing. "Hold it. What's going on here?" Ms. Kirby said.

Dave poked the snake with his foot. "Rubber," he said.

"What is all this about?" Ms. Kirby demanded.

"I...h-hate sn-snakes," Donna stammered.

"Someone's been playing a practical joke," Dave said slowly.

"Did you do it, Joel?" Ms. Kirby asked.

Joel was still laughing, but he shook his head.

"How many people know you don't like snakes, Donna?"

"Everyb-body." Donna looked at Dave for help.

"You want me to tell?" he asked.

She nodded.

"See, last year in Mr. Tomas's class, we had to act out famous scenes from history," Dave said. "Ginger Janowitz decided to do Cleopatra's death. From under her jacket she pulled out her pet boa. Donna took one look at it and ran screaming from the room. Joel had to go get her. But she wouldn't come back until Ginger and the snake left."

"I just saw Ginger and her father," Ms. Kirby murmured, almost to herself. "Ginger was nowhere near this room."

Oh, yes she was, thought Dave. But he decided to share that information with only one other person: Sam.

3

"So, Ginger...*huff*...played a...*huff*...joke on ...*huff*...Donna," Sam said as he did twenty-five jumping jacks. "You're not...*huff*...going to... *huff*...squeal, are you?"

"Of course not," Dave answered, leaning back against the headboard of his bed. "You know me better than that."

"Then what's...*huff*...bothering you?"

"I don't know. Something's wrong. Ginger was coming out of the room. And she wasn't carryng anything. There was nothing she could've had the snake in."

Sam stopped jumping and sat down, facing Dave, at the foot of the bed. "Maybe she had it in a paper bag and she threw that away in the wastepaper basket."

"But her father was with her. He'd wonder..."

"Maybe she told him it was her leftover lunch...."

Look, Dave, what's the big deal? Even if Ginger didn't do it, even if somebody else did it, it was just a practical joke, right? It wasn't serious."

"No, it wasn't serious. But, I don't know, I have this funny feeling something's out of whack."

Sam looked solemnly at his brother. He respected Dave's funny feelings just as Dave respected his. "What do you want me to do?" he asked.

"Nothing. Yet," answered Dave.

4

Sam agreed to help build the scenery as well as work the lights. He liked measuring, sawing, pounding and painting. He got as much pleasure from seeing a finished set as Dave did from the audience's applause. But this set looked a little more complicated than the others he'd worked on.

"A ship?" Sam asked Mr. Matthius, the art teacher in charge of set design, as they sat on the stage. There wasn't any rehearsal that day—just a meeting of the technical crew, including Mary Ellen, who wanted to be up on all aspects of the production. "A real ship with cannons?"

"Well, just part of a ship," Mr. Matthius said.

"But it's got to be sturdy enough to stand on," Mary Ellen put in. "And the cannons are fake."

"We're going to need a lot of wood then," a girl named Claire said.

"Not very much—just for a platform. The rest of the ship will be made of cardboard. I'll show you how it can be done," said Mr. Matthius.

Everyone on the crew, including Sam, looked at each other as if to say, "Oh, yeah?"

As they were leaving, Mary Ellen stopped Sam. "Uh...Sam...I want to ask you something." She shifted her bag from one shoulder to the other.

Sam immediately shrank back. Mary Ellen had had a crush on him the year before, had followed him around and even sent him poems. He'd been embarrassed by the whole thing and avoided her a lot until he found out she thought he was Dave. Then it struck him as hilarious. Fortunately, by that time, Mary Ellen had gotten tired of running after the Bean brothers and had given up. At least, Sam hoped she had.

He held his breath, waiting for her question, and when it came—"Aren't you...uh...good friends with Luis Melendez?"—he gave a sigh of relief. Then he thought about the question. He wasn't really tight with Luis, but they played on the same ball team—in fact, they were two of the best players on it, Luis being a good pitcher and Sam a top-notch catcher and hitter—and they hung out to-gether sometimes.

"Not close friends," he answered. "Why?"

"Well, his father's a reporter for WPRY and I

thought maybe he'd do a feature about my play—
you know, interview the cast, the director, me. To
stir up some interest before we open."

WPRY was the local television station and Sam
didn't think that Luis' father, who presented stories
about the illegal dumping of chemicals near the
county reservoir and organized crime in the real
estate business and who was something of a local
celebrity, would be interested in featuring a dinky
school play. But he didn't say anything.

Mary Ellen plowed right on. "I thought maybe
you could mention it to Luis and Luis could talk to
his father."

Sam didn't reply.

Mary Ellen tapped her foot. "Well, will you?"

"I...uh...don't think...er," stammered Sam, back-
ing away. "Luis' dad reports on more...um...dra-
matic things."

"My play is dramatic."

"More exciting and important things."

"My play's exciting and important."

"Look," Sam finally blurted out, "if the cast
came down with a weird disease or the Mafia busted
up the scenery, that would be exciting and important and maybe he'd be interested. But otherwise..."

"That's not exciting, that's sick. He should write
about happy things, good things—not just awful
ones. My play's good, really good."

"Yeah. Right. Well, I've got to go, Mary Ellen."
Sam hurried out.

"It is good. You'll see. Everybody'll see," Mary Ellen called after him.

5

At the next rehearsal, Ms. Kirby checked Donna's desk and script, even though Donna had had it in her knapsack all day.

"All clear," she said. "Now, I want to start working on Act I, scenes i and ii. Dave, Mary Ellen, Donna. You read."

"*'Bonjour,* Fifi...'" Dave began.

But he was interrupted by the appearance of Ginger Janowitz. "Can I speak with you, Ms. Kirby?" she asked.

"What is it, Ginger?" asked Ms. Kirby, sounding annoyed.

"Well," she lowered her voice. "I have this idea. Most actors have stand-ins—you know, someone to take their place in case they get sick or hurt or something. So I wondered—well, I'd like to be Donna's stand-in."

"That's a nice idea, Ginger, but we could use you much more on the crew."

"My dad said I could do both, Ms. Kirby. Please."

At the mention of Mr. Janowitz, Ms. Kirby winced. "Well, all right. You can be the stand-in, then."

"She just better not bring her snake with her," Donna muttered.

"Don't worry, I'll fight it off with my trusty sword," said Joel.

Donna giggled.

"All right, Sir Hugo," said Ms. Kirby. "Please start again."

Dave picked up his script. "'*Bonjour*, Fifi. Is your mistress in?'" he read.

Mary Ellen answered with her line, "'*Oui, oui*.'"

"Said this little piggie," Joel snorted.

Everyone laughed except for Mary Ellen and Ms. Kirby. "That's enough from you, Joel," said the director, "if you want to be in this play."

"I don't want to be in this play," Joel mumbled. "I want to be in *Grease*."

"Continue, Mary Ellen," Ms. Kirby said, ignoring him.

"'I weel fetch her,'" Mary Ellen said.

"Brigitte comes downstairs into the drawing room," Ms. Kirby read the stage directions.

"What are they drawing?" said Joel.

Ms. Kirby threw him a look.

"'Ah, Miss De Tour,'" said Dave.

"'Sir Hugo, what brings you to my humble abode?'"

"'I am going away, Miss De Tour. Far away. I am going to hunt for pirates.'"

"'Pirates!'"

"'Yes. Jean La Fleet and his men have been terrorizing the seas for too long. I am being sent by the king to capture them.'"

"'But Sir Hugo, Jean La Fleet is a dangerous man.'"

"'Very dangerous,'" Dave read. "'That is why I'm asking you, Miss De Tour...dear Brigitte...if you will give me your promise to marry me should I return alive.'"

"Hot stuff," Joel murmured.

"Shhh," said Ginger.

And then, the fire alarm rang. Everyone jumped and laughed.

Dave saw Donna turn around and give Joel a conspiratorial look.

"Since when do we have fire drills after school?" Ginger demanded.

"Since we've had after-school activities," Ms. Kirby said. "Now, no more talking. Leave your scripts on the desks and get into line."

Outside the school, Donna stood next to Dave and whispered, "I've got this idea. If we all refuse to act in Mary Ellen's dumb play—you know, strike—maybe Ms. Kirby will let us put on something else."

"Forget it," Dave whispered back. "Ginger will get your part and some other people are sure to get mine and Joel's."

"Where is Joel?" Donna asked innocently, glancing around the street.

Dave looked around too—in the street, at the

school. His eye caught something at the window of the rehearsal room. It was Joel's face. Then it abruptly disappeared.

Donna noticed Dave's stare and followed it. "He's up there? He's doing it." She snapped her fingers.

"No talking," Ms. Kirby rapped out. Then she sneezed and reached for her handbag. "Oh, heavens, I've left my purse on my desk. How careless of me," she exclaimed. "Mary Ellen, will you make sure it's safe?"

"Is that legal, Ms. Kirby, going into the school during a fire drill? I mean, I don't want to get into trouble," said Mary Ellen, who wouldn't be caught dead without her purse.

"I'll tell Mr. Bryant. If anyone tries to stop you, send him or her to me."

"Okay," Mary Ellen said dubiously. She reentered the school.

Then Ms. Kirby asked, "Where's Joel?"

"Right here, Ms. Kirby."

Dave did a double take, but Joel just grinned at him.

The fire drill ended and Ms. Kirby led the group back in the school and up to the rehearsal room.

"Everything okay, Mary El...?" Ms. Kirby stopped.

Amid a pile of crumpled, torn pages, Mary Ellen was slumped on the floor. In each of her hands was a mangled script. She looked ready to cry.

"What is the meaning of this? Who did this?"

Mary Ellen shook her head miserably and held out a piece of paper.

Ms. Kirby took it and read aloud, "'*The Merry Pirates* ought to walk the plank.'" She shook her head, crumpled the note and threw it into the wastepaper basket. "This is not a mere practical joke. This is malicious. Now, who did this?"

"It couldn't have been any of us, Ms. Kirby," one of the girls said. "We were all outside for the fire drill."

Without being obvious, Dave stole a glance at Joel. This time he wasn't grinning.

6

The school newspaper, *The Dart*, ran a small article on the destruction of the scripts. A lot of people tried to guess who had done it, but no one really knew. Except Dave (and Sam). But Dave didn't mention the incident to Joel. He was waiting to see whether or not Joel would confess. Dave did, however, manage to fish the note the vandal had left from the garbage. He thought it might be useful evidence. Ms. Kirby chalked up the incident as an unsolved mystery and made copies of the script from the original, which Mary Ellen had, luckily, left at home.

And so for a few weeks, nothing else happened to mar rehearsals of *The Merry Pirates*. Then, one day, while Sam was hammering away on the platform of the ship for the play, he felt eyes staring at him and looked up to see Ginger Janowitz, smiling.

"I'm working on the crew today," she said. "Mr. Matthius said you need help getting the sets ready. He said you'd show me what to do."

"Okay," Sam said. "See, there are two sets—the ship, which is going to be used for both Sir Hugo's vessel and the pirates' ship, and the drawing room. We've got this painted backdrop with this real sofa, chair and coffee table in front of it and this chandelier hanging down. That's the drawing room."

"I get it. Then you move out the furniture, lift the backdrop, and there's the ship," Ginger said.

"Right."

"Great. Let's get to work. What do I do?"

"Um...you could start by screwing the light bulbs in that chandelier Mr. Matthius just hung up."

"Okay."

An hour later, Mr. Matthius said, "I've got to leave, kids. Put everything away and don't tell anybody I left before you did."

As the crew began to straighten up, Mary Ellen came in. Ginger greeted her, "Oh, hi, Mary Ellen. You're still here?"

"Yes. I have to keep an eye on everything. You crew members are doing a good job."

"*Cast* and crew members," said Ginger.

Mary Ellen gave Ginger a sympathetic look. "Cast and crew," she repeated. "I'm sorry you won't get to act the part of Brigitte."

"Oh, you never know, Mary Ellen. I may get to be in your play. Donna could break her arm or something. You never know.... Well, I've got to get home. See you tomorrow." Ginger left.

Slowly, Sam picked up his and Ginger's tools and put them away. The rest of the crew left.

"Even though Ginger wants the part so much, I hope nothing does happen to Donna. She's a much better actress than Ginger," Mary Ellen said. Then she looked over the set and sat down on the old velvet sofa Joel's mother had lent them for the play. "This is really coming along. We're going to rehearse on this set tomorrow, you know."

"I know," Sam said. "I'm going to be there to make sure everything's okay."

"What do you mean?" Mary Ellen asked sharply.

"To make sure the set's right."

"Oh. Of course."

"Well, 'bye, Mary Ellen."

"'Bye."

Sam left her sitting on the sofa, dreamily running her hand over the cushions.

7

"*'Bonjour*, Fifi. Is your mistress in?'" Dave was saying.

Sam sat there, trying not to laugh. This play really is dumb, he thought. But he admired the way Dave had thrown himself into the part, acting every inch an English nobleman—slightly stuffy, rather imperious. He also enjoyed watching Donna, who had made an entrance like an African queen, or the way Sam imagined an African queen would make an entrance.

Ginger, who was sitting next to him, obviously wasn't enjoying Donna's entrance as much. "Big ham," she muttered under her breath, and sniffed.

Dave and Donna sat on the sofa.

"Hold it. That sofa's not in the right place. Did somebody move it?" Ms. Kirby asked.

She's right, thought Sam.

"I think it looks good there, Ms. Kirby," Mary Ellen called from the wings.

Ms. Kirby ignored her. "Sam, will you reposition it?"

Sam climbed on stage and, with Dave's help, shoved the couch back into place directly under the chandelier.

"Good. Now Brigitte and Sir Hugo, continue," Ms. Kirby said.

Sir Hugo proceeded to propose marriage to Brigitte.

Then Donna said, "'I cannot believe you wish to marry me. I am neither beautiful nor rich.'"

"'You are rich enough for me,'" Dave said, kneeling at Donna's feet.

"Stop. The line is 'You are beautiful enough for me.'"

Everyone laughed. Dave winked at Sam, then said, "Oh, sorry," and repeated the line correctly.

"'Then marry you I will,'" said Donna.

"'Oh, my dear Brigitte,'" Dave said, kissing her hand.

"Smack, smack. Mush, mush," said Joel, kissing his own hand loudly.

"That's enough, Joel," Ms. Kirby ordered.

"He's just asked her to marry him and he's kissing her hand?" Joel sneered.

"Sir Hugo is very formal," Mary Ellen said, entering. "Ms. Kirby, I really think that sofa..."

"Jeez." Joel sighed.

"Fifi, just say your line and don't worry about the sofa," Ms. Kirby said.

"'Your coach eez waiting, Sir Hugo,'" said Mary Ellen.

Dave and Donna rose and moved stage left toward the wings.

"Hold it. Something doesn't look right," said

Ms. Kirby. "Take it from the proposal once again and let me see what's wrong."

"Again?" Donna sighed and rolled her eyes.

"Again."

"I can do it if she's too tired, Ms. Kirby," Ginger called out.

"Ginger, dear, stand-ins should be present, but not heard from." Ginger slumped back down in her seat.

Dave and Donna returned to the sofa. As Sir Hugo proposed once more, the rest of the cast and crew, sitting in the audience, began to fidget and talk among themselves. All except Sam, whose attention was caught by a slight movement above Dave and Donna's heads. The chandelier was swaying slightly. But there was no breeze.

Mary Ellen entered once again and said her line. But Sam didn't notice her. His eyes were riveted to the chandelier, which had begun to shiver and swing in a wider arc.

Dave stood up. "'Farewell, dear Brigitte.'"

Donna began to rise. "That's it. I've got it," said Ms. Kirby. "Turn to him, Brigitte, but don't get up. Stay on the sofa—like a proper lady."

"'Farewell, Sir Hugo,'" Donna said.

"Look out!" yelled Sam, springing up.

Donna jumped up just as the chandelier crashed to the floor, missing her by two inches.

In the wings, Mary Ellen screamed.

Dave ran over to Donna to make sure she was all

right. He was joined by Sam, Joel and the rest of the actors and crew.

Donna was very, very quiet.

"Are you okay? Donna, say something," Joel insisted.

"Wow. Maybe it's a good thing you have a stand-in," said Steve, one of Sir Hugo's "men."

Donna slowly stood up. "I don't need a stand-in," she said, "because I quit." With great dignity, she walked off the stage.

Everybody turned to Ginger.

"I'll go and speak with Donna," Ms. Kirby said. "But if I can't convince her not to quit, it looks as though you'll have to play the part, Ginger."

Nodding her head, Ginger tried—and failed—to hide her triumphant smile.

8

"That chandelier falling wasn't an accident. I checked the cord. It was cut. Donna could've been badly hurt. You could've been too," Sam said as he and Dave walked home from the ill-fated rehearsal. They'd hung around as long as they could looking for clues until Ms. Kirby made them go. "But I think Donna was the one who was supposed to get it. Dave, it has to be Ginger. You saw her near the rehearsal room before the snake business. Then she got to be the stand-in. Yesterday, she put light bulbs in the chandelier and said to Mary Ellen maybe she'd get to be in the play if something happened to Donna. Something almost did. Somebody better talk to Ginger—even though now that she's gotten the part she won't be pulling any more nasty tricks."

Dave shook his head. "No. Something's wrong." He was quiet for a minute. "What about the scripts?"

"The ones that got ripped up? You said Joel did that. To try to sabotage the play. Besides, someone left a note then. There wasn't a note this time, so it was probably a different person with a different motive."

"Let's go over to Joel's."

"Right now?"

"Yes. He lives on the next block."

Sam shrugged, but followed Dave to Joel's house.

Joel let them in. He looked pretty upset. It was no secret he liked Donna a lot. "I'm going to wallop that Ginger," Joel said.

"What makes you think she had anything to do with it," Dave said coolly.

"Who else would've?"

"It might've been an accident."

"Humph," Joel said. But it was obvious that he was wondering about it.

"Actually, we've come to talk with you about

something else," Dave continued smoothly. "Remember this?" He pulled out the note Ms. Kirby had thrown away.

"Yeah. It was with the ripped-up scripts. So?"

"Did you rip them up?"

"Wait a minute. That was weeks ago..."

"I was hoping you'd confess and I wouldn't have to rat."

"Confess? Confess what? I didn't tear up those scripts. Sure, I think the play stinks, but I wouldn't do anything as nasty as that."

"I saw you. At the window. And Donna did, too. She said, 'He's doing it.'"

Joel snickered. "Oh, so that's it."

Dave and Sam waited for the explanation.

"Yeah. I *was* in the rehearsal room."

"Why?" asked Sam.

"I guess I can tell you now. It was a bet I made with Donna. That next time there was a fire drill I'd hide in the room and then sneak down to the street once everybody was out without being caught. Donna said I couldn't do it. But I did."

Dave stared hard at Joel. Then he said, "Okay, were the scripts in one piece when you were there?"

"Yes. They must've been ripped up after I left and before Mary Ellen went into the room."

"Hmmm."

"Why is this important now, anyway? You guys playing detective or something? Even if I had ripped up the scripts, they're only paper. It's Ginger you

should be talking to if you really want to be private eyes. She tried to hurt a person—two people even. You could've been hurt, too."

"Don't worry. We'll talk to Ginger," Dave said. "See you tomorrow, Joel."

They left him frowning on his stoop.

"Do you believe him?" Sam asked as he and Dave continued toward their house.

"Yeah. I think so."

"Well, so maybe someone else did rip up the scripts just to be mean. But so what? Joel's right. We should talk to Ginger. She tried to hurt Donna and maybe you."

Suddenly, Dave stopped dead on the sidewalk. "No. No one wanted to hurt either of us."

Sam stopped too and stared at his brother. "Huh? A chandelier with a cut cord almost landed on Donna's head, and you say no one wanted to hurt her?"

"The sofa was moved. If Ms. Kirby didn't have such sharp eyes and hadn't insisted we move it back to its original position, Donna and I would have been nowhere near the chandelier when—and if—it fell."

"You're right. But I don't get it.... Wait.... Maybe Ginger was just trying to scare Donna into quitting and not hurt her. And it worked."

"Maybe. But I'm not sure."

They walked up the steps to their house.

"Then what *do* you think is going on?" asked Sam.

"I don't know yet. But we better both keep our eyes open because I think *The Merry Pirates* are still in for stormy seas."

9

The kids in the cafeteria were talking about the chandelier incident. And not just the cast and crew either. *The Dart* had printed a big second page article with the headline: ACTRESS QUITS PLAY: "SOMEONE'S OUT TO GET ME," SAYS DONNA JORDAN.

"Wow," Sam heard one girl say. "I think I'm gonna have to see this play. Who knows what might happen."

"Aww, this chandelier business was just an accident," a boy said.

"That's not what Donna thinks."

Dave brought his tray over to his brother. "We're getting some publicity."

"Yeah," agreed Sam, glad he wasn't performing. "There's Mary Ellen. She doesn't seem too happy."

Looking miserable, Mary Ellen joined them. "I'm going to get ulcers from this mess," she said.

Sam and Dave glanced at each other. Sometimes Mary Ellen sounded forty years old.

"People keep saying somebody's trying to wreck the play," she said, "but that's ridiculous. Just because a chandelier fell down..."

"And some scripts got torn up. And a fake snake was put in Donna's desk," added Dave.

Mary Ellen sighed.

Sam and Dave didn't say anything.

The silence was broken by a loud voice demanding, "Did you see this?" Ginger Janowitz, waving a copy of *The Dart*, sat down next to them. "That... that *person* practically accused me of trying to brain her. That's...that's..."

"Libel," said Dave. "If it isn't true."

"What do you mean, 'if'? Don't tell me *you* think I had anything to do with this."

"You did get her part," Sam said.

"I would never do anything so low to get a part. Any part," Ginger said.

"What about putting a snake in the desk of someone who's afraid of snakes?" Dave asked.

But Ginger had already left in a huff.

10

"Hey, how's it going, bro," Luis Melendez called.

"Okay," answered Sam.

"Want to catch a few?"

"Sure."

Luis wound up and threw a beautiful fast ball that smacked neatly into Sam's glove. Sam sent it back and Luis next pitched a slider that was out of the strike zone. "Let me try that one again," he said.

The ball whistled perfectly through the air. Sam caught it and grinned.

"Hey," Luis said. "I gotta tell you something funny. My dad was looking at *The Dart* last night. Have you seen it? That interview with Donna Jordan? She talked about the snake business and someone ripping up the scripts and then the chandelier falling. You're on the crew of that play, *The Jolly Pirates* or whatever it's called, aren't you? Well, my dad said to let him know if anything else happens. He says news is a little slow these days and it might make a good bit for his show. He'd like to interview Ms. Kirby and the author, what's her name?"

"Mary Ellen Moseby."

"Right. Well, tell her my dad might want to interview her."

"Okay," said Sam. "I'll tell her."

11

Ms. Kirby couldn't convince Donna to return to the play, so Ginger got the role of Brigitte. Dave didn't think her acting was as good as Donna's, but it wasn't terrible and at least she was lively. The rest of the cast was more jumpy than lively. Mary Ellen went around clutching her purse even tighter. Joel didn't crack any jokes. And the other actors avoided standing under any hanging props. Ms. Kirby tried to calm them down, but she didn't succeed. And there was only one week to go before opening night.

The crew was faring better. Nothing had happened to any of them and so they went about their business, finishing the ship, which looked wonderful, right down to the *papier-mâché* cannons.

"Let's try the last scene of the play," Ms. Kirby said at the next rehearsal. "On the ship this time."

It was the first time the cast had seen the complete set and they were impressed. They walked around, admiring the curved cardboard bow, touching the cannons, checking out the big sails that rose into the flies. Then they took their places, which Ms. Kirby adjusted and corrected.

"Okay, remember, no scripts now. Your lines should be memorized. And Mary Ellen, please leave your bag backstage. I'm sure no one will take it. Okay, Sir Hugo, begin."

"'Sink me, if it's not Jean La Fleet, the pirate king,'" said Dave.

Fencing foil (borrowed from his brother) in hand, Joel defiantly faced him. "'The same. And your wish, Sir Hugo, is my....' What's that?" Joel's nose twitched.

"Now what?" asked Ms. Kirby. "We haven't even gotten through three lines of dialogue."

"That smell," Joel said.

"Phew!" "What is that?" "Did something die in here?" "It smells like skunk," voices said.

"Somebody's at it again," moaned Mary Ellen.

"It's getting worse," Ginger complained.

"I'll call the custodian," Ms. Kirby said. Then she coughed. "Oh, dear, it is getting worse. Maybe we'd better wait outside while Mr. Landers finds out what's causing it. Quickly now. Follow me."

"Good idea," said Ginger.

Dave thought he'd never seen a teacher move so fast as he watched Ms. Kirby, handkerchief over her nose and mouth, rush out of the auditorium. She was followed by the gagging, sputtering cast.

All except Dave. With his own handkerchief tied over his face, he began to explore the stage. As he neared the cannon, the smell got so strong he had to fight off being sick. Slowly, he lifted the light barrel off the cannon. Something rattled to the floor. Dave stooped to pick it up. It was an empty, uncapped little bottle with a scrap of paper wrapped around it. Dave removed the paper and looked at the label on the bottle. "Eau de Skunk." A novelty store specialty. Then he read the note. "This is what I think of the play," it said.

On his way out of the auditorium, Dave met Mr. Landers, the custodian. "P.U.," said Mr. Landers. Dave showed him the bottle. "The only thing that'll clear up that smell is a couple of gallons of tomato juice. But I guess we'll have to settle for air freshener." He lumbered toward the stage with a spray can.

Dave left the building. Ms. Kirby was outside with the cast and a couple of other after-school activities teachers and groups of students who'd been evicted by the smell wafting up to their classrooms.

"Ms. Kirby," Dave said.

"One too many incidents," she was telling Mr. Tomas.

"Ms. Kirby," Dave repeated, louder this time.

Ms. Kirby glanced at him. "Just a minute, Dave. I'm busy."

Dave frowned and looked around. Ginger was still holding her nose. Mary Ellen was still clutching her shoulder bag and looking dazed. Joel was nowhere to be seen. But there was another familiar face. Donna Jordan.

"Hi, what are you doing here?" Dave asked.

Donna looked embarrassed. "I...we...I...came to...I want my part back."

"Will Ms. Kirby give it to you?"

"I...I don't know...I....Hey, who's that....Isn't he..."

A red Volkswagen pulled up in front of the school and a dark-haired, familiar-looking man got

out, followed by a thin woman with a video camera. He came up to Dave and Donna. "Excuse me," the man said. "Geraldo Melendez of WPRY. I got a tip that there are some interesting goings-on here today over a school play."

"Who gave you the tip?" Dave asked boldly.

"It was anonymous. Sounded like a kid, but could've been an adult with a high voice. Could have been male or female. Anyway, Anonymous said to talk to Mary Ellen Moseby and Ms. Alice Kirby."

"I'm...uh...Mary Ellen Moseby," a small voice said.

Geraldo Melendez turned around. "Pleased to meet you," he said. "Now, what's this about somebody trying to sabotage your play."

As Mary Ellen began to speak, Ms. Kirby motioned Dave over. "Is that Geraldo Melendez?" she asked, primping her hair.

Dave nodded.

"What is he doing here?"

"He got tipped off that someone is trying to sabotage the school play."

"Sabotage. That's a strong word."

Silently, Dave held out the bottle and the note.

Ms. Kirby read them. "This is the last straw," she said. "Someone has been playing one prank too many."

"Would you tell our viewers who you think the culprit is?" Geraldo Melendez asked Ms. Kirby. He

had just walked over with the camerawomen and Mary Ellen.

"I have no idea," Ms. Kirby said coolly. "But either we catch this person soon or I'm canceling the play before someone gets hurt."

"Oh, no," moaned Mary Ellen.

Oh, yes, thought Dave.

12

On television that night, Geraldo Melendez presented a feature on *The Merry Pirates* mishaps. There were Mary Ellen and Ms. Kirby a foot high on the screen. "Despite the general air of tension hanging over the play, the brave cast continues to rehearse *The Merry Pirates*," the reporter said. "But they wonder, what will happen next? Alice Kirby, the director, has threatened to cancel the production if the saboteur isn't caught. That would be a sad finale to so much hard work."

"Saboteur? Boy, is he slick," Sam said, watching the show.

"Uh-huh," agreed Dave.

"So what are we going to do? How are we going to catch this 'sab-o-teur,'" Sam asked, pronouncing the word carefully.

"WPRY urges the culprit to stop these senseless

acts," Geraldo Melendez continued. "He or she can have nothing to gain from destroying the efforts of such a talented band of youngsters. This is Geraldo Melendez for *Scoop*. Good night."

Sam was silent for a long time. Then he asked, "Who *do* you think is doing it, Dave? Joel? Ginger? Donna?"

"Donna?"

"You said you saw her today and she wants her part again. Maybe she was trying to get back at Ginger."

"She wouldn't drop a chandelier on her own head and she couldn't have ripped up the scripts. She was with me," said Dave.

"I still think someone else ripped up the scripts."

"No. Look, here's the note that was left that time and here's the note I found today. Same handwriting. Same person."

"But there was no note when the chandelier fell," Sam said. "Maybe that was Ginger, and somebody else ripped up the scripts and put the Eau de Skunk in the cannon."

"I don't know. I don't think there were two different saboteurs. Maybe there *was* a note with the chandelier and it got misplaced or swept up in all that glass," Dave said. "It's gotta be somebody in the cast, though, who used the skunk juice. Nobody else was near that cannon. I think it's a question of motive. I think there's a motive that makes all the incidents make sense."

"Somebody hates the play."

"Maybe...or..."

"Or?"

Dave shook his head and sighed. "I don't know. I'm stumped. Have you got any ideas?"

"No," said Sam.

Dave sighed again. "This sure is a tough case to crack."

"Yeah. You can say that again."

13

All during the following week, Sam and Dave were especially on their guard, watching for any signs, big or little, of further sabotage, but they saw nothing and nothing happened. However, instead of the tension among the cast members easing, it grew. "If anything else is going to happen, I bet it'll be during dress rehearsal," Dave heard Joel tell Donna, who'd gotten her part back.

Ginger was furious at Donna, at Ms. Kirby, and also at Dave, since he'd questioned her about the chandelier incident. She wouldn't talk to him. Joel was being cool toward Dave too, and because he was, so was Donna. And so Dave was feeling a little unhappy himself.

Sam felt sorry for his brother. He didn't have to

work with all those people, so the tension didn't affect him quite so much. He kept his mouth shut and his eyes open.

Geraldo Melendez did another report on the play, which made the atmosphere even heavier. He announced on the air that ticket sales for the The Merry Pirates had outstripped all school play sales in the county for the past thirty years, surpassing even those for the 1965 production of Bye-Bye, Birdie, starring the then local celebrity, Mitzi Moon. "Everyone seems to be wondering what might happen on opening night," the reporter said. "Will the pirate ship blow up? Will any of Sir Hugo's crew walk the plank and not return for the curtain call? Excitement is running high. The public loves disasters and, just like in ancient Rome, will pay plenty to see them."

"Boy, is that irresponsible journalism," Dave fumed. "If the saboteur was running out of ideas, Geraldo Melendez just gave him or her a few more."

"Word has it that two amateur detectives, Sam and Dave Bean, are investigating the mystery. WPRY wishes them good luck. This is Geraldo Melendez for *Scoop*. Good night."

"Now, how'd he find *that* out?" asked Sam.

"Who knows, but so much for undercover work," said Dave.

14

On the afternoon of the dress rehearsal, Sam decided to check the lights he'd be working that evening. They'd had a "tech" rehearsal the day before—a rehearsal to make sure the lighting and sound cues and set changes were right—and the lights were fine then, but Sam had one of his funny feelings. As he rounded the corner to enter the lighting booth, he heard a strange click. He looked around, but, in the dark, he saw nothing. He flipped on the small bulb over the lighting board. Everything looked okay. One by one he flicked the switches.

Another click. This time it sounded like a door being shut.

Sam ran out through the wings. The stage door was closed, but on the ground in front of it was a piece of paper. It read, "Stay out of spying, Bean Brothers, and nobody will get hurt." The saboteur was here! Sam flung open the stage door and ran down the corridor. Too late. Whoever had left the note was gone. Darn, he thought. Slowly, he walked back to the lighting board. *Flick. Flick.* The spotlights were fine. Then he turned on the strobe, the flickering light that would add an old movie qual-

ity to the fight scene. It flickered on and then died out. Sam began to turn on the other switches. Dead. All the lights were dead except the bulb in the booth itself. Sam grabbed a flashlight that was handy and checked the wires under the board. Then he checked the fuse box. So that was the game. Someone had fiddled with the lights so that when the strobe's switch was pulled, it would overload the circuits and blow all the lights. Someone who didn't want Sam to check the lights before the rehearsal. He rested his chin on his hand. Then, whoosh, something lit up inside his head, and he knew exactly what he had to do to catch the saboteur. All he needed was Dave's help.

15

In his black costume, three-cornered hat and with a red scarf around his neck, Joel looked very piratical. He seemed to be a little more excited than usual, too. He kept leaping at Dave and yelling, "*En garde*, British swine!"

"Take that, French *cochon*," Dave answered back, having learned the French word for "pig" from his mother.

Donna looked great in her striped dress, very pretty and elegant—even though Ginger, with a tight smile on her face, claimed she looked like a circus tent.

Mary Ellen, still carrying her purse, but wearing the frilly apron and cap of Fifi the maid, looked more nervous than ever.

"All right," said Ms. Kirby. "Places, everybody. Act I, scene i."

"Did she say Axe I, scream i," whispered one of the girls in the cast.

A few people giggled.

Then the scene began. The act, with its two scenes, went as well as could be expected, with only a few corrections from Ms. Kirby.

The cast took a break.

"Anybody check the cannons tonight?" Joel asked Dave.

He nodded. "No problems."

"How about the chandelier?"

"It's safe, as far as I know."

Joel shook his head. "You still think I had someting to do with it, don't you?"

Dave looked Joel straight in the eye. "I'll answer that question at the end of this rehearsal."

"Okay, Sir Hugo the Great." Joel kicked at the bow of the ship and walked away.

Dave sighed and hoped Joel would still talk to him after the case was solved.

Ms. Kirby called, "Places for Act II." The play moved along through Brigitte's capture by the pirates to the climactic final scene—the fight between

Sir Hugo and Jean La Fleet, after which Brigitte chooses the pirate king as her husband. "'*En garde,*'" said Joel. Dave raised his sword. The lights went down and the strobe flickered on. But after a few seconds, it died out. The stage was completely black.

"Lights! Where are the lights?" yelled Ms. Kirby.

Somebody screamed.

"Who's that?" a voice called.

"Me, Lois," said another.

"What was that?"

"You stepped on me."

Then, *pow, pow, pow!* Red sparks. The smell of gunpowder. Something was exploding on stage. Shrieks and scuffling feet. "Ahh!" "Let's get out of here!" "Hurry!"

"Stay where you are, don't pan..." Ms. Kirby called.

Pow! Crack! Fizz!

More screams.

And then, suddenly, the stage was flooded with light.

"Hold it," commanded Dave. "Put out that firecracker."

Everyone turned confusedly to look at him, then followed his gaze to...Mary Ellen Moseby.

"You!" Joel yelled.

"Mary Ellen! You're the last person we ever suspected," shouted Ginger from the audience.

"Have you been doing all this stuff—the snake,

the scripts, the chandelier and the cannon?" asked Donna.

"Not the snake," Mary Ellen said, looking at Ginger, who was suddenly sheepish.

"I had it in my pocket to give to my sister and I thought... Well..." Ginger's voice faded out.

Dave and Sam, who'd come on stage, looked at each other and shrugged.

Then Ginger said, firmly, "But I never tried to drop a chandelier on Donna's head."

"That was an accident," said Mary Ellen. "It wasn't supposed to fall near anybody. That whole thing was a mistake. The note I wrote wasn't found. What a mess."

Ms. Kirby looked shocked. "But why, Mary Ellen, why you, of all people?"

"I think I can answer that," Dave said. "For publicity. Isn't that right?"

In a tiny voice, Mary Ellen said, "I didn't want to hurt anybody. When the chandelier nearly hit Donna, I almost called my whole plan off. But after the article in *The Dart*, I decided to go on with it, only to try to be more careful. Dave's right. I did do it for the publicity." Then, with a gleam in her eye, she said, louder, "And it worked."

16

"So when I realized somebody had messed with the lights so there'd be a blackout, I decided to pretend there was one. That way the saboteur could do whatever she was going to do. But I'd fixed the lights so I could turn them on when I wanted to," Sam explained to Ms. Kirby after everyone else had gone.

"Yeah, and he told me about it. My job was to stay put and keep an eye on the stage when the lights went on," said Dave.

"That was good work. I bet Geraldo Melendez will want to interview you two," Ms. Kirby said.

Geraldo Melendez did. Sam and Dave got even more publicity than the play. As for that, word had leaked out that the saboteur was Mary Ellen Moseby and that no more sabotage was going to take place. Word also leaked out that *The Merry Pirates* was, in Sam and Dave's mother's words, a "real stinker." The second night's audience was as small as it had been for all of Mary Ellen's other plays. For Mary Ellen Moseby, crime only paid for a short time.

"Guess what," Joel said to Dave and Sam at the cast party. "Ms. Kirby told me we can do *Grease* next year. So much for Mary Ellen's original dramas."

"Great. Although I have to admit I do feel kind of sorry for Mary Ellen," said Dave.

"But not sorry enough to be in another one of her plays, I bet," said Joel.

"No, not that sorry." Dave grinned, happy that he and Joel were friends again.

Donna joined them. "Oh, my dear Sir Hugo, you're an even better detective than you are an actor."

"And that's not saying much," teased Joel. "Nah, just kidding. Actually, I think both of you guys have got a swell career ahead of you."

"You said it. I can see the sign on their office now," Donna put in. "Bean Brothers, Detectives."

"Bean Brothers, Private Eyes," Sam spoke up.

Dave turned to his brother in pleased surprise. "Hey, I like that: Bean Brothers, Private Eyes."

"I thought you might," said Sam. "I thought you just might."